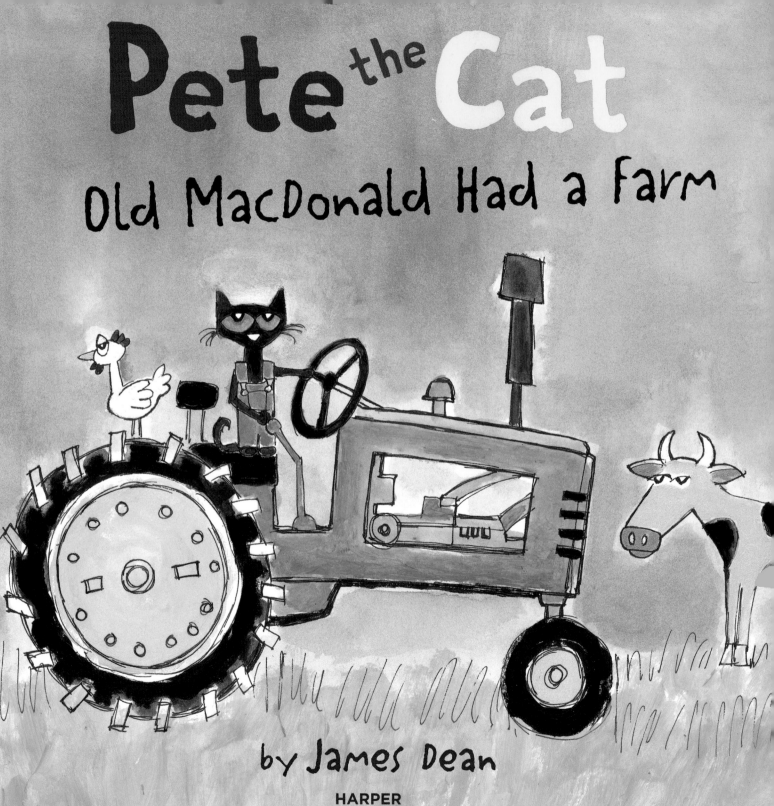

Pete the Cat

Old MacDonald Had a Farm

by James Dean

HARPER

An Imprint of HarperCollinsPublishers

Pete the Cat: Old MacDonald Had a Farm
Illustrations copyright © 2014 by James Dean
All rights reserved. Manufactured in the United States of America.
No part of this book may be used or reproduced in any manner whatsoever without written
permission except in the case of brief quotations embodied in critical articles and reviews. For
information address HarperCollins Children's Books, a division of HarperCollins Publishers, 195 Broadway,
New York, NY 10007.
www.harpercollinschildrens.com

ISBN 978-0-06-219873-0 (trade bdg.)

The artist used pen and ink, with watercolor and acrylic paint, on
300lb hot press paper to create the illustrations for this book.
Typography by Jeanne L. Hogle
14 15 16 17 18 PC   10 9 8 7 6 5
❖
First Edition

Old MacDonald had a farm, E-i-e-i-o!
And on that farm he had some chickens, E-i-e-i-o!

With a cluck-cluck here,
And a cluck-cluck there,
Here a cluck, there a cluck,
Everywhere a cluck-cluck,
Old MacDonald had a farm,

E-i-e-i-o!

Old MacDonald had a farm, E-i-e-i-o!
And on that farm he had some dogs, E-i-e-i-o!

With a woof-woof here,
And a woof-woof there,
Here a woof, there a woof,
Everywhere a woof-woof,
Old MacDonald had a farm,

E-i-e-i-o!

Old MacDonald had a farm, E-i-e-i-o!
And on that farm he had some cows,
E-i-e-i-o!

With a moo-moo here,
And a moo-moo there,
Here a moo, there a moo,
Everywhere a moo-moo,
Old MacDonald had a farm,

E-i-e-i-o!

Old MacDonald had a farm, E-i-e-i-o!
And on that farm he had some pigs, E-i-e-i-o!

With an oink-oink here,
And an oink-oink there,
Here an oink, there an oink,
Everywhere an oink-oink,
Old MacDonald had a farm,

E-i-e-i-o!

Old MacDonald had a farm,
E-i-e-i-o!
And on that farm he had some horses,
E-i-e-i-o!

With a neigh-neigh here,
And a neigh-neigh there,
Here a neigh, there a neigh,
Everywhere a neigh-neigh,
Old MacDonald had a farm,

E-i-e-i-o!

Old MacDonald had a farm,
E-i-e-i-o!
And on that farm he had some cats,
E-i-e-i-o!

With a MEOW-MEOW here,
And a MEOW-MEOW there,
Here a MEOW, there a MEOW,
Everywhere a MEOW-MEOW,
Old MacDonald had a farm,

E-i-e-i-o!

Old MacDonald had a farm,
E-i-e-i-o!
And on that farm he had some goats,
E-i-e-i-o!

With a **baa-baa** here,
And a **baa-baa** there,
Here a **baa**, there a **baa**,
Everywhere a **baa-baa**,
Old MacDonald had a farm,

E-i-e-i-o!

Old MacDonald had a farm, E-i-e-i-o!
And on that farm he had some ducks,
E-i-e-i-o!

With a quack-quack here,
And a quack-quack there,
Here a quack, there a quack,
Everywhere a quack-quack,
Old MacDonald had a farm,

E-i-e-i-o!

Old MacDonald had a farm, E-i-e-i-o!
And on that farm he had some turkeys,
E-i-e-i-o!

With a gobble-gobble here,
And a gobble-gobble there,
Here a gobble, there a gobble,
Everywhere a gobble-gobble,
Old MacDonald had a farm,
E-i-e-i-o!

Old MacDonald had a farm, E-i-e-i-o!
And on that farm he had some roosters,
E-i-e-i-o!

With a cock-a-doodle here,
And a cock-a-doodle there,
Here a cock-a-doodle,
there a cock-a-doodle,
Everywhere a cock-a-doodle,
Old MacDonald had a farm,

E-i-e-i-o!

Old MacDonald had a farm, E-i-e-i-o!
And on that farm he had some donkeys,
E-i-e-i-o!

With a hee-haw here,
And a hee-haw there,
Here a hee-haw, there a hee-haw,
Everywhere a hee-haw,
Old MacDonald had a farm, E-i-e-i-o!

Old MacDonald had a farm, E-i-e-i-o!
And on that farm he had some sheep, E-i-e-i-o!
With a maa-maa here,
And a maa-maa there,
Here a maa, there a maa,
Everywhere a maa-maa,
Old MacDonald had a farm, E-i-e-i-o!

Old MacDonald had a farm,
E-i-e-i-o!
And on that farm he
had some frogs,
E-i-e-i-o!

With a ribbit-ribbit here,
And a ribbit-ribbit there,
Here a ribbit, there a ribbit,
Everywhere a ribbit-ribbit,
Old MacDonald had a farm,

E-i-e-i-o!

Old MacDonald had a farm, E-i-e-i-o!
And on that farm he had some geese, E-i-e-i-o!

With a **honk-honk** here,
And a **honk-honk** there,
Here a **honk**, there a **honk**,
Everywhere a **honk-honk**,

Old MacDonald had a farm,

E-i-e-i-o!